C.1

E R
SCH

Schade, Susan

Toad takes off

DUE DATE

| | | | |
|---|---|---|---|
| | | | |
| | | | |
| | | | |
| | | | |
| | | | |
| | | | |
| | | | |
| | | | |
| | | | |
| | | | |
| | | | |

## A NOTE TO PARENTS

When your children are ready to "step into reading," giving them the right books is as crucial as giving them the right food to eat. **Step into Reading Books** present exciting stories and information reinforced with lively, colorful illustrations that make learning to read fun, satisfying, and worthwhile. They are priced so that acquiring an entire library of them is affordable. And they are beginning readers with a difference—they're written on five levels.

**Early Step into Reading Books** are designed for brand-new readers, with large type and only one or two lines of very simple text per page. **Step 1 Books** feature the same easy-to-read type as the Early Step into Reading Books, but with more words per page. **Step 2 Books** are both longer and slightly more difficult, while **Step 3 Books** introduce readers to paragraphs and fully developed plot lines. **Step 4 Books** offer exciting nonfiction for the increasingly independent reader.

The grade levels assigned to the five steps—preschool through kindergarten for the Early Books, preschool through grade 1 for Step 1, grades 1 through 3 for Step 2, grades 2 through 3 for Step 3, and grades 2 through 4 for Step 4—are intended only as guides. Some children move through all five steps very rapidly; others climb the steps over a period of several years. Either way, these books will help your child "step into reading" in style!

*For Andy Schroeder,*
*who says that flying low*
*is the most fun.*

Copyright © 1997 by Jon Buller and Susan Schade. All rights reserved under International and
Pan-American Copyright Conventions. Published in the United States by Random House, Inc.,
New York, and simultaneously in Canada by Random House of Canada Limited, Toronto.

http://www.randomhouse.com/

*Library of Congress Cataloging-in-Publication Data*
Schade, Susan. Toad takes off / written and illustrated by Susan Schade & Jon Buller.
p.  cm. — (Step into reading. A Step 1 book)
Summary:  Although he cannot fly like the birds, Toad finds a way to take to the air.
ISBN 0-679-86935-2 (pbk.)  —  ISBN 0-679-96935-7 (lib. bdg.)
[1. Toads  Fiction. 2. Animals  Fiction. 3. Airplanes—Piloting—Fiction. 4. Stories in rhyme.]
I. Buller, Jon, 1943–   II. Title.  III. Series: Step into reading. Step 1 book. PZ8.3.S2871q 1997
[E]—dc20 96-8773
Printed in the United States of America 10 9 8 7 6 5 4 3 2 1

STEP INTO READING is a registered trademark of Random House, Inc.

Step into Reading®

# TOAD TAKES OFF

By
Susan Schade
and Jon Buller

A Step 1 Book

Random House 🏠 New York

I am a Toad.
I don't know why
ducks can swim
but Toads can't fly.

# I dive.

# I float.

I watch the sky.

I see the ducks

gliding by.

I hear a roar.

I see a plane.

An idea pops

into my brain!

An airplane ride!

I'll go right now!

I'll take my friends

Pig and Cow!

At Eagle Airport,

I park the car.

Look how many
planes there are!

Warbirds, racers,
ultralights!

# Where do we go
# for scenic flights?

Our pilot's name
is Captain Dick.

Check the controls,

*click, click, click.*

Then turn the key.

The propeller whirs.

*Puckita, puckita,*

the engine purrs.

Roar down the runway,
faster and faster,
straight for the fence
and TOTAL DISASTER!

N363

Sixty miles per hour.

Pull back on the stick.

We swoooooooop
off the ground!
Way to go, Captain Dick!

Over the trees,
up in the air,

I see my pond,
my house, my chair!

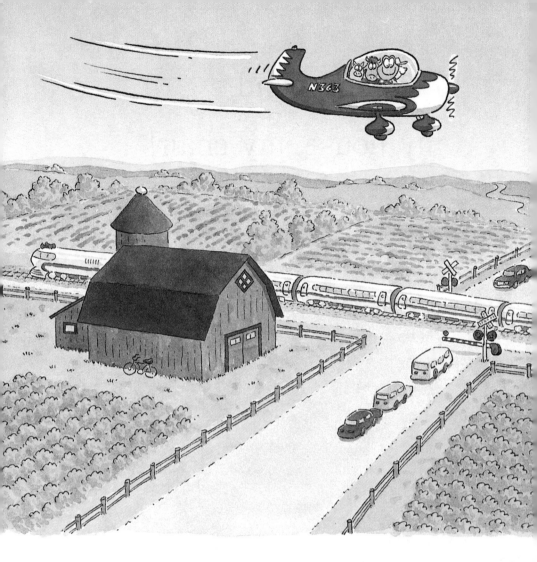

We see Cow's barn
and her bike out back.
We see the road
and a train on the track.

We fly up the river
to see Pig's boat.

We circle over
Pup and Goat.

We buzz the school.

We climb up high.

We bank. We cruise.

We ride the sky.

Dick says, "You try!"
He shows me how.

Look out, birds!

# Toad's flying now!